What it was like to be a ...

# VIKING

## DAVID LONG

Illustrated by
**Stefano Tambellini**

Barrington Stoke

First published in 2023 in Great Britain by
Barrington Stoke Ltd
18 Walker Street, Edinburgh, EH3 7LP

www.barringtonstoke.co.uk

A CIP catalogue record for this book is available
from the British Library upon request

ISBN: 978-1-80090-212-1

Printed by Hussar Books, Poland

*For Leopold "Pop" Scott*

# CONTENTS

# 1

# STRANGERS FROM AFAR

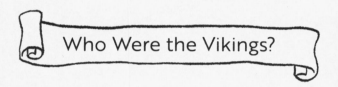

## Who Were the Vikings?

In the eighth century, Europe was a very different place to live compared to today. The countries we know didn't exist more than a thousand years ago, and hardly anyone went to school. People belonged to tribes instead of nations, or they lived in small kingdoms ruled by powerful chiefs and kings.

Each population was much smaller too. There were probably only around two million people living in the whole of the British Isles, for example, compared to nearly 70 million today.

The people in what we now call Scandinavia were mostly blue eyed and often had blonde or reddish-brown hair. They were called Norse or Vikings. Norse probably relates to Norway, but experts still don't agree where the name "Viking" comes from or what it really means. Viking men are mostly shown in films as bearded warriors with horned helmets. We see them sailing across the sea in vessels known as longships to attack members of other tribes.

Some of the Vikings did do this. Many of their most spectacular treasures were stolen

from other tribes in violent and bloodthirsty raids. Anyone they captured alive became a slave. But the Norse people weren't all bloodthirsty warriors, and none of them fixed horns to their helmets.

Most Vikings lived peaceful, normal lives. They loved poetry and telling stories as they sat around roaring fires at night. They made beautiful works of art out of stone and metal and by carving animal bones and antlers. The Vikings also began the world's oldest surviving parliament, where they voted to make laws and settled any arguments they had between themselves.

Many of the most famous Vikings were incredible explorers and adventurers. They sailed thousands of miles in their beautifully designed longships. Both men and women risked their lives crossing the Atlantic Ocean to settle in new lands. Other Vikings worked as traders and merchants, travelling almost as far as the sailors did.  They exchanged goods and ideas with people from the ancient empires of Europe, Asia and Africa.

All this helped the Vikings to develop a rich and fascinating culture.  What became known as the "Viking Age" lasted for nearly 300 years, and it has captivated archaeologists and historians ever since.

# 2

# DAWN TO DUSK

Life on a Viking Farm

The Vikings were descended from Stone Age people who had migrated to land on the other side of the North Sea from Britain. They lived in the area which is now covered by the countries Norway, Sweden and Denmark. To begin with, most of these people were fishermen and farmers who lived in small settlements rather than towns or cities.

Families built their farms close to rivers and forests because people needed fresh water to survive and firewood for cooking and heating their homes. Wood was also used to construct fences to stop any farm animals from wandering off or being stolen by a rival tribe.  A strong wooden fence protected everyone from the wolves, bears and vicious wild boars living in the surrounding countryside.

## A Viking Longhouse

Fire for cooking and heating

Area for animals

Thick walls made of mud or clay

Most Vikings lived in rectangular buildings called longhouses, which had thick walls made of timber and mud or clay. There were no glass windows, so the houses were often built to face the sun. That way they got as much natural heat and light as possible.

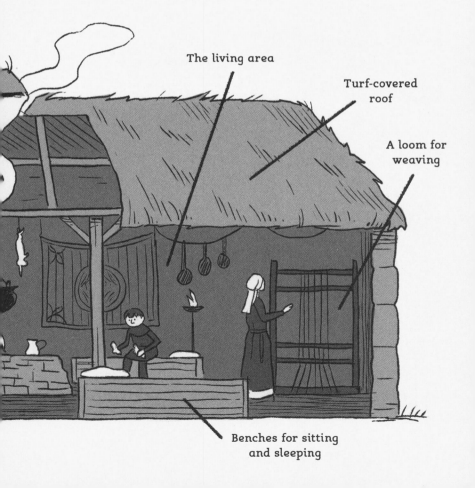

The living area

Turf-covered roof

A loom for weaving

Benches for sitting and sleeping

The roofs were often covered in turf – thick slices of earth and grass that were cut from the ground and then laid on top of the longhouses like large floppy tiles. Turf gave the houses excellent protection from the wind and rain, and could be easily replaced if necessary.

The longhouses weren't often very big – just a single room with space at one end for the family and space at the other for animals. Cows, pigs and chickens all lived inside with the adults and children when the weather got really bad. The smell from the animals must have been awful for the humans. The only heat came from a fire and from the animals' hot, steaming dung.

The fire was lit in the centre of the longhouse. It filled the house with smoke because there was no proper chimney. The fire was used for cooking meals such as stewed meat and vegetables. Everyone in the family slept as close to it as possible when the weather turned cold.

The children slept on wooden benches or on piles of a dried plant called heather. These were much softer than sleeping on the floor, which was made of mud that had been stamped on and beaten flat.

No one had any privacy, and there was no toilet or bathroom. All this meant life in a crowded longhouse was very basic and pretty uncomfortable. Men, women and children all kept clean by washing themselves in nearby streams or by using cold water they collected in homemade wooden buckets.

The villagers got meat and milk from their farm animals, and honey from bees. Wool and leather from the animals were used to make clothes, belts and shoes. The honey helped to sweeten food, as there was no sugar in this part of the world back then.

Each farm had to produce enough food for everyone who lived in the longhouse. This generally included grandparents as well as the mother and father and all their children. For much of the year the animals needed to be fed too, as the weather meant they couldn't graze in the fields.

It was hard work to grow this food and care for the animals, because the climate in Scandinavia is much harsher than it is in the rest of Europe. Winters are long and often bitterly cold, and in the far north the sun doesn't even rise above the horizon for several weeks.

A lot of the work on the farms was done by the children and their mothers and grandmothers, who did everything by hand. The men were often away at sea for weeks at a time or out hunting wild animals.

Crops had to be planted, watered and then harvested. The pigs, cows, sheep and chickens all needed to be fed and stopped from running away. Vegetable gardens had to be kept free of weeds, and any fish that were caught were smoked over the fire or packed in salt. This was a smelly job, but it preserved the fish so the family could store it and eat it to survive the cold, dark winter.

The children also helped around the house every day. They made sure the fire stayed alight and cleaned out the animals' end of the building when the stink got too bad.

Harvesting crops

Children tending
the fire

Feeding
animals

Weaving

Preserving
fish

Another important job was grinding grains between flat stones to make porridge or the flour needed to bake bread.

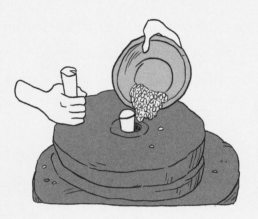

The grains came from crops called oats and rye and sometimes wheat. Vikings also grew barley, which was used to brew a type of beer.

Other important jobs for the children included gathering firewood and spreading the animals' dung on newly planted crops to help them grow. Firewood was needed all year round in the longhouse, and the children might also find fruit or berries that could help feed the family while looking for sticks and fallen branches.

None of the boys or girls ever went to school, but they were taught lots of practical skills such as lighting a fire, rowing a boat, and how to spin wool and weave it into cloth.

These young Vikings still found time to play despite being kept busy with work for much of the day. They had board games and wooden dolls, footballs to kick around and toy sailing boats.

Archaeologists have also discovered whistles made from the bones of geese at sites where Vikings used to live. These whistles

are hollow like straws. Another noisy toy
the Vikings had was called a "hummer". This
was carved from pig bone and threaded onto
a cord. Then it could be spun round a child's
head to make a spooky humming sound.
Animal horns were also used to make musical
instruments, and several examples of these
have been found in old Viking settlements.

Strangely, Viking children didn't have
surnames like we do. Instead, a child's second
name was usually the father's name with "son"

or "dottir" (meaning "daughter") joined on to the end. It was very rare for children to be named after their mother, so a girl called Frida with a father called Harald was known as Frida Haraldsdottir. Her little brother Leif would be called Leif Haraldsson.

Sadly, many Viking children died when they were still very young. This wasn't unusual in the eighth century, when there weren't any doctors. People died easily – even a small cut could turn poisonous and kill a person. Historians now think one out of every five Viking children died before their fifth birthday, and around a third never grew up to become an adult.

Even the people who did survive rarely reached what we think of as old age. Vikings thought people were old when they were only 40, and hardly anyone lived to be 50 or 60.

# 3
# UNRAVELLING THE MYSTERY

Religion and Writing in Runes

The life of a Viking sounds difficult, but the farms could also be lively, bright places with noisy feasts and celebrations.

The Vikings had to make their own clothes, but these were often colourful because they knew how to make natural dyes from wild plants and roots. These included species such as woad, madder, hedge bedstraw, tansy and knapweed.

Many of these plants were found growing in the countryside around the farms. Their

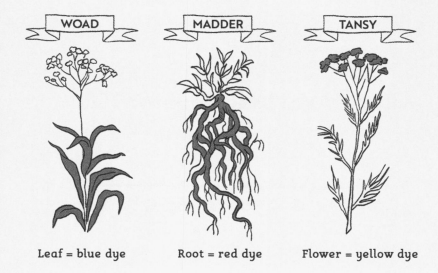

WOAD

MADDER

TANSY

Leaf = blue dye     Root = red dye     Flower = yellow dye

beautiful colours made it possible to dye cloth, such as that woven from sheep's wool, different shades of blue, red, orange, yellow and green. They also dyed linen, which was made from another plant called flax.

Blue was the most popular colour, but the plants used for dyeing only grew at certain times of year, just like the crops that were grown for food. Finding the right plant was another job that children could help with, but everything had to be picked at the correct time.  This meant the Vikings had to understand the different seasons.  Feasts and festivals were often held in the villages to mark the change from one season to the next.

We don't know much about what happened at these festivals, but we do know that Viking children and their parents didn't celebrate Christmas or Easter because they weren't Christian.  Vikings were pagans like many of the people living in northern Europe at this time.  This meant they worshipped lots of different gods.  Viking children were taught that the gods lived in a mysterious place called Asgard and that each god was responsible for certain things in life.  Vikings also believed that the gods could help humans in times of trouble.

Odin was the god of wisdom and war.  He was the most important Viking god and rode a ghostly grey horse called Sleipnir, which had eight legs for extra speed.

Thor was the god of thunder and lightning and had a chariot pulled by hairy goats. He was much stronger than any human. Thor defended Asgard with a magic hammer called Mjolnir against enemies such as giants and evil trolls. When Thor threw Mjolnir, it came back to him like a boomerang. Many Vikings wore small copies of Mjolnir as jewellery, believing that this would mean Thor would protect them too.

Frey made crops ripen and children grow tall. When a Viking man and woman got married, they hoped Frey would help them have lots of strong, healthy children. The Vikings also had important goddesses. Frigg was the Queen of Asgard, whom they believed protected mothers and new babies.

However, gods could be bad as well as good. One of them called Loki was thought by many Vikings to be half-god, half-devil.

**ODIN**

God of War

**FRIGG**

Goddess of
Fertility

**THOR**

God of Thunder
& Lightning

**FREY**

God of Peace
& Fertility

**FREYA**

Goddess of Love
& Fertility

**HEL**

Goddess of the
Underworld

**LOKI**

God of Mischief

**BALDUR**

God of Light
& Purity

**BRAGI**

God of Music
& Poetry

**NJORD**

God of Wind
& Sea

Viking children learned about gods like Loki and Frigg by listening to long poems and exciting adventure stories called sagas. These sagas were spoken aloud by storytellers because the Vikings didn't have books to write them down in.

The best storytellers travelled around from village to village. Their stories and poems were passed from one generation to the next by being told and retold over hundreds of years. They were made up, like other legends and fairy tales, but modern historians can learn a lot about the lives of real Vikings by studying these sagas.

The Vikings didn't read or write books, but they had a form of writing which used special marks called runes.

The letters were made up of lines, which had to be straight because runes were designed to be cut into wood or bone or stone.

The lines were arranged vertically or at a sharp angle because carving a horizontal line on a piece of wood can make it split or snap, and curved letters take much longer to carve into a hard surface.

The word "rune" means "secret" in the Norse language, which is funny because things written in runes can look a lot like the codes spies use to send secret messages. The runes had many different uses including forming part of Viking magic and spells. They have also been found carved on gravestones and at ancient religious sites.

Other runes were scratched onto personal possessions, such as a name tag showing who owned an item. Runes on a piece of solid gold or silver jewellery often spelled out the name of the person who made it.

Viking sailors left examples of runic graffiti in some of the places they visited. These have been found all over Scandinavia as well as on Scottish islands and in several settlements dotted around the Anglo-Saxons' kingdoms which later joined to become England. A runic inscription was carved onto a piece of tree bark that was discovered thousands of kilometres away in Russia. It showed that some land there once belonged to a very well-travelled Viking called Visgeirr.

Most runic inscriptions are short, but they can still be useful to the people who study Viking history. Decoding ancient runes helps historians to learn a lot about Viking communities. Runes have also provided clues about some of the amazing trips made by Viking sailors, and about the importance of the pagan religion and its rituals to the Vikings.

# 4

# THE VILLAGE WORKSHOP

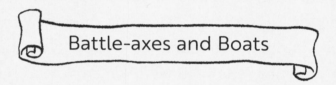

Battle-axes and Boats

Some of the Vikings worked as highly skilled craftsmen instead of farmers or fishermen. People known as smiths worked with metal and had one of the most important jobs in the village. They made things the local families needed as well as other items that could be sold or traded with villages elsewhere in Scandinavia and on trips overseas.

Many of the items smiths made were practical things such as iron pots and pans for cooking in the longhouses. They also made belt buckles, tools for farming, weapons and

even scissors. The raw materials came from something called bog iron, which could be found lying around locally or from rocks called ore that were dug up. The metal these rocks contained was dirty and impure. It had to be melted in something called a furnace before the iron could make anything useful. When ore is melted, it is called "smelting".

A Viking furnace was a type of oven made of clay mixed with sand and dung. It was about a metre high and looked a bit like a circular

chimney. The temperature inside could reach more than a thousand degrees centigrade, so smelting iron was very dangerous work. It wasn't a job for small children, but some of the stronger ones must have been taught how to do it as they grew older.

Smelting bog iron and ore in a furnace took many hours, but the Vikings became experts at it. Their best smiths could produce metal of a very high quality, and the things they made in their workshops became some of the Vikings' most valuable and treasured possessions.

Useful items like scissors were used for cutting cloth and shearing sheep, but possibly also for trimming the beards of Viking men. The way a person looked was very important, and the heroes of their sagas were often described as being handsome or beautiful.

We know that many of them owned tweezers for plucking out bristles and unwanted hairs. Some even had tiny scoops for cleaning out their children's ears. Other craftsmen made combs and toothpicks out of animal bones and deer antlers.

The best furnaces could be used to produce a type of steel as well as iron. Steel is a much harder metal, and it lasts longer than iron, which makes it perfect for helmets and weapons such as swords and daggers. Steel is made by mixing molten iron with a natural substance called carbon.

Village smiths sometimes put bones into their furnaces with the ore and bog iron. These included human bones as well as animal ones. They did it because pagans believed the spirits of the dead would make the blades of their battle-axes and swords stronger and even sharper.

They soon found that this worked, but it was because of science not magic. It worked because bones contain lots of carbon – carbon makes up nearly a fifth of every human. If the furnace was hot enough, the carbon in the bones could change ordinary iron into stronger, harder steel.

This discovery meant that Viking swords, knives and axes were some of the best in the world, but the smiths made many other things too. They used gold for their most precious creations, as well as silver and also bronze, which is a mixture of two cheaper metals called tin and copper.

These metals were used to make highly decorated boxes and beautiful jewellery, such as bracelets, brooches and rings. The Vikings also made armbands and neckbands called torques, which were very popular. Their jewellery was often worn to bring good luck, by men as well as women. We know this because a lot of it was buried with the owners when they died.

Swords, shields and spearheads were also buried in this way. Modern archaeologists have been able to study many fine examples following discoveries of metal goods alongside skeletons in ancient Viking graves.

Other smiths, who were probably younger and less skilled, spent their time making massive quantities of iron rivets. These are a bit like little nails and were used in shipbuilding. The Vikings were the best shipbuilders in the world at this time, and hundreds of rivets were needed to fix wooden beams and planks together to make each new vessel.

The rivets were much easier to make than a sword or gold and silver jewellery, but the work must have been very boring because so many of them were needed every year. Some of the older children may have helped to make them as part of their training in a smith's workshop.

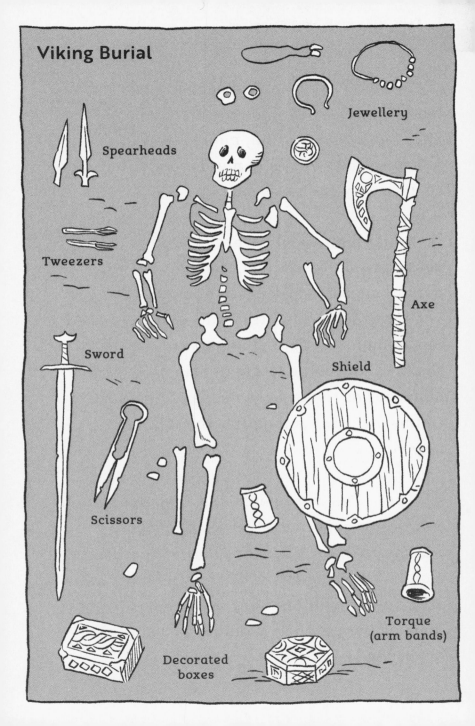

# Viking Burial

Spearheads

Jewellery

Tweezers

Axe

Sword

Shield

Scissors

Torque
(arm bands)

Decorated
boxes

The Vikings built their ships out of oak, ash, elm or pinewood. They were so good at it that these boats began to change the way the Vikings lived. Their boats weren't just elegant and well made. They were also brilliantly designed to work in many different situations, and the Vikings fast became Europe's most skilful sailors.

A Viking longship could cross hundreds of miles of open ocean. It could do this quickly because the hull was slim and streamlined, which made it very fast. It was also so strong that it could withstand the battering of the waves and the terrible storms that happen all the time out at sea. These must have been dangerous and uncomfortable voyages for the sailors, as there were no cabins on board a longship where they could shelter.

Longships had oars as well as a sail, and they were narrow to ensure they could travel along even small rivers. This was essential if the captain and his crew wanted to travel inland rather than just sailing up and down the coast. Their sleek hulls could move around in fairly shallow water.

Even the largest longships were light enough for the crew to carry them short distances overland if a river was blocked or impassable. Sailors used ropes made of twisted horsehair or strips of dried walrus skin to carry the longships.

The size of the vessels varied, but most longships were around 20 metres long – about the same length as four family cars.  Each longship had between 24 and 50 oars, and the 40 to 50 crewmen sat on wooden chests to row.  The chests contained the crew's personal

## Viking Longship

Figurehead

Oars

possessions and any food they needed for the voyage. A special long oar at the back right was used to steer the boat. It was called a styrbord, which is where the word "starboard" comes from – meaning the right-hand side of a vessel.

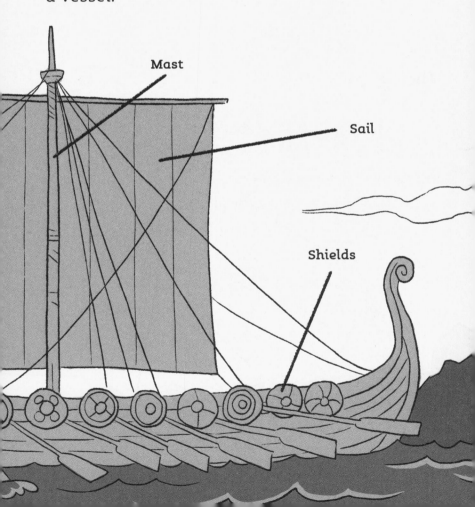

Mast

Sail

Shields

# 5

# SETTING SAIL

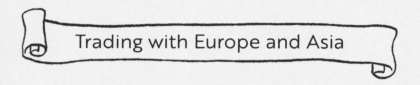

Trading with Europe and Asia

When the Vikings first set sail at sea, it was
as traders and merchants. To begin with,
many of them travelled overseas in slightly
wider vessels known as knarrs. A knarr could
be operated by a much smaller crew than a
longship. Sometimes only six or seven sailors
were needed, and this left more space on board
for the goods they hoped to trade when they
reached their destination.

The Vikings were very good at making
things, but there were items which they
couldn't make or find in Scandinavia. These

included luxurious Chinese silk cloth, which was popular among the very rich Vikings who could afford to wear it. The traders also wanted wine, exotic spices, glass, crystal beads and silver coins that were melted down to make more jewellery.

A lot of trade in Europe at this time involved barter or exchange, rather than buying and selling with money as we do now. To pay for the goods they wanted, the traders filled their knarrs with things they could swap, such as animal skins, furs, iron and tin, weapons, walrus ivory and whalebone.

They also took along small amounts of honey-coloured amber, a precious type of fossilised tree-sap or resin that is used to make jewellery. Most traders had scales on the boat to weigh the pieces of silver they swapped for their amber and other goods.

It might seem strange to us now that anyone would melt silver coins down for jewellery instead of spending them. But perhaps the most surprising thing is how far these Vikings were prepared to travel to get the things their customers wanted.

In the eighth century, long-distance travellers had none of the clever navigating equipment that we all take for granted now. Sailors on the knarrs didn't have magnetic compasses or even maps, so they steered using

the sun and stars as a guide. Sailing a boat
west towards the sunset meant it was headed
for Britain. Sailing east towards the sunrise
told a Viking he was on his way home to
Scandinavia.

This might sound easy, but these journeys could be very long.  In the chilly sea around Scandinavia it is very often cloudy and foggy, meaning no one could see the sun or the stars.  The crews usually stayed as close to the coast as possible to avoid getting lost.  Unfortunately, this could also be dangerous, as knarrs were often wrecked on the rocks.

A crew needing to travel a much longer distance had no option but to brave the open ocean.  Navigating became harder and harder as the voyages got longer.  A ship's captain probably had to rely on somebody looking out for wildlife to tell him where they were.  Spotting a seal swimming or a seabird is one way to know that you are getting close to land.

The crews were all male, at least to begin with, so the women and children stayed behind to look after their farms.  As the voyages got longer and longer, many of these vessels must have sunk, killing everyone on board.  But other crews were lucky and able to complete their journeys safely, landing on a beach somewhere in Britain or France. Once on dry land, these sailors began trading with the people they found living in the nearby villages.

Some voyages took the Vikings even further than this, however. We now know that Vikings travelled as far west as Ireland to trade some of their goods, as well as reaching parts of the Middle East. In this way they began to create a trading network that covered many distant regions of the world.

This brought the Vikings into contact with Christians and Muslims and people from many other cultures. Several modern European cities began as trading points before developing into large settlements. Dublin and Kyiv were both important Viking trading towns centuries before they became the capitals of Ireland and Ukraine.

The Vikings' longer voyages needed
larger vessels than the original knarrs. They
developed a type of longship called a karve,
which took more time to build and was more
expensive than a knarr. But it could carry
many more goods on each voyage. As a result
the Vikings' impressive trading network
continued to grow. Some Viking traders began
travelling up long rivers that stretched deep
into Russia, while others headed south to the
Mediterranean and on towards the coast of
Africa.

Evidence of the Vikings' extraordinary
expeditions has been found all over the globe,
from Iraq in the Middle East to the frozen
wastelands of the Canadian Arctic. Historians
know of many examples of Viking goods being
transported thousands of kilometres before
they were exchanged. Archaeologists have
also discovered jewellery and other luxuries
in Viking graves that could only have been
obtained from faraway lands.

At least one Viking owned jewellery made of an old solid silver coin from Iran. The tomb of another Viking contained metalwork manufactured in the Middle East as well as religious items from northern India.

An English man and his father were using a metal detector when they discovered a collection of 600 coins hidden beneath the ground at a secret site in Yorkshire in 2007. This fabulous treasure was found in an ancient pot made of Viking gold and silver, and the coins turned out to be from Russia, Afghanistan, Africa and Samarkand in central Asia.

Very few Vikings ever owned this much treasure, but many of them left other clues when they reached new places.  These may not sparkle like gold or silver, but they can be just as interesting.

Some Swedish historians were very excited to find runes carved into the stonework of Turkey's most important mosque, the Hagia Sophia, dating back 1,500 years.  Unfortunately, they were too worn down to be decoded, but the runes on a sculpture of a lion in the Italian city of Venice are bit clearer.  However, no one knows exactly who carved these runes, and it's possible that the vandal was a Viking soldier rather than a trader or merchant.

Fascinating ancient documents have also been discovered that were written by Muslims living in Spain and Russia at this time.  These were written in Arabic, and they describe the meetings the Muslims had with Viking travellers.  One of them went to a

Viking funeral and another rudely described the Vikings he met as "the filthiest of God's creatures". It is impossible to know whether they really were. All we can say now is that they were all a very long way from home at a time when travel was difficult and very dangerous.

# 6

# RAIDERS NOT TRADERS

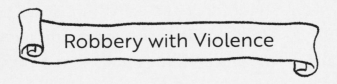

Robbery with Violence

A few Vikings became enormously rich as a result of their skill as traders. But before long, others started to realise there was a much easier way to get the things they wanted – they could just steal them from other people.

These thieves were called raiders, and Britain was their most obvious target. It was closer to Scandinavia than most other countries, and the Vikings were already used to making the journey across the North Sea. In good weather with a strong wind, such a voyage could take just four or five days.

The largest longships had room on board for dozens of heavily armed warriors. At first these raiders also had the element of surprise on their side, and this made the early raids even more shocking for their victims.

People living near the coast in Britain had got used to foreign visitors arriving on nearby beaches. For years Vikings had come to trade but now, suddenly, it was impossible to know whether a vessel spotted offshore contained friends or enemies. No one could be sure what was happening until the crew had actually jumped out onto the beach – and by then it was often too late to fight back.

The first Viking raid we know about was on the south coast of England and occurred towards the end of the eighth century. The exact year is unknown, but three Viking ships set sail for the kingdom of Wessex, and their crews landed in a part of it that we now call Dorset. A small group of Anglo-Saxons went down to the beach to greet the visitors, but they were immediately attacked and killed.

The Vikings returned to their ships after committing these shocking acts and quickly sailed away.  This turned out to be the first of many similar raids.  The next one was even more violent.  It took place in the year 793 at Lindisfarne, a rocky island off the coast of Northumberland.

The tiny island was home to some Christian monks who lived in a religious community called a monastery.  The monks themselves were all poor, but monasteries like the one on Lindisfarne were often very rich. Christians liked to give their local monastery gifts of money and valuable objects if they could afford to, believing that giving generous gifts would help them get to Heaven.  However, the Vikings were pagans not Christians, so they just saw the monastery as an opportunity to get rich.

It was an easy target for a band of heavily armed warriors. Many of the monastery's most precious items were small enough to carry away on a longship, such as gold or silver candlesticks.

The monks who lived in the monasteries weren't very good at protecting themselves, and they were extremely unlikely to have any weapons to help them chase the Vikings away.

Also, monks often lived on islands or in quiet, isolated places by the coast. This meant the crew of a Viking ship could sail up to a monastery, rob it of all its valuables and then sail off again before anyone else in the area realised what was going on.

The sight of some longships approaching the beach must have been terrifying, but the ships themselves would have looked magnificent.

Many of the longships had ornately carved dragon or snake heads fixed to the pointed prow at the front of their hulls.  Rows of brightly painted wooden shields hung along each side of the vessels and their billowing sails were often dyed blood-red.

But these were clearly ships built for war, and the men on board all carried swords and axes when they scrambled onto the beaches. Most of the Vikings had played with swords when they were children.  It was part of their training to become fighters.

In June 793, the Lindisfarne raiders didn't just brutally murder the monks who came down to the beach to meet them.  They also stole everything of value that they could carry away from the monastery, and they killed all the cattle.  A report described afterwards how the island's church was spattered with the monks' blood and stripped of all its furnishings.

The same thing happened about a year later at a monastery in Jarrow, which was further down the coast.  Not long afterwards, another island community was attacked, at Iona in Scotland.  Later, two more monasteries further along the coast from Jarrow were raided.  Iona was attacked another three times and by the end completely destroyed.  Monks began reporting that similar raids were taking place in parts of Ireland.

By the beginning of the ninth century, it was clear that the Viking raids were getting larger and even more violent. They were also happening more often, and large numbers of local people were being captured and taken away as slaves. The sudden appearance of a fleet of longships on the horizon would strike fear into the heart of any man, woman or child who saw it.

# 7

# WAR AND CONQUEST

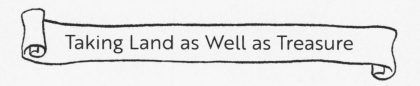

Taking Land as Well as Treasure

The Vikings continued raiding in this way for several years before changing their tactics. The monasteries and small settlements on the coast had been easy targets, but once they had all been attacked and burned a few times, there was very little treasure left for the Vikings to steal.

A few raiders had begun attacking fairly large towns instead, but now they decided to use their military power to grab land as well as steal valuables. These Vikings wanted farms and farmland as well as gold and silver.

Once again, they planned to take these by force while capturing as many people as they could to sell as slaves.

In the year 865, the Vikings began to gather their largest ever fighting force back home

in Scandinavia. The Anglo-Saxons called it the Great Heathen Army and must have been terrified of the rumours they had heard about it, despite not knowing how many thousands of warriors were joining the army or the names of the leaders.

The Vikings' plan was very clear.  The huge army was intended to invade rather than raid, and it was heading across the North Sea to take over the Anglo-Saxon kingdoms of East Anglia, Northumbria, Mercia and Wessex.  The Vikings wanted to conquer these regions so they could live in them instead of just sailing home after stealing whatever they could from the monks and their neighbours.

A large fleet of longships was needed to carry so many warriors.  It took many months to get over a hundred vessels together, but eventually the longships were completed and ready for the voyage.  The heavily armed Viking fighters climbed aboard them and set sail.

The Anglo-Saxons were naturally horrified when the fleet was spotted a few kilometres off the coast of East Anglia.  Probably none of them had ever seen so many vessels before, and by this time they knew that the men on board weren't sailing across the North Sea simply to trade.

The Anglo-Saxons also knew that they didn't have enough soldiers to defend themselves against so many warriors. Once the longships had landed, the Anglo-Saxons tried desperately to persuade the Vikings to go back home to Scandinavia. This had sometimes worked in the past with some of the raiders. Smaller Viking gangs had occasionally agreed to leave the kingdoms alone if the Anglo-Saxons paid them enough money to leave.

This money to get rid of the Vikings was called Danegeld, but it didn't work this time. Now the Vikings said they weren't interested in money, but they did agree to a more unusual deal. The army's commanders said that if the Anglo-Saxons gave them hundreds of horses, they would leave East Anglia alone and attack one of the other kingdoms instead.

This looked like a good deal for the local Anglo-Saxons despite horses being very expensive animals in the ninth century. But it was terrible news for everyone else. If the Viking army was equipped with horses, its men could travel faster and further inland. Warriors on horseback are also much harder to fight because they can strike down soldiers on foot using their swords and axes.

The Anglo-Saxons agreed the deal, and after resting in camps over the winter, the Great Heathen Army left East Anglia and cheerfully headed north. Before long the Vikings had killed the king of Northumbria and captured the large and important city of York. They renamed it Jorvik and made it their capital, which was a terrible blow to the Anglo-Saxons.

Next the army attacked the kingdom of Mercia. Its king managed to escape, but the Vikings took over the town of Nottingham, which at that time was called "Snotingeham". They quickly turned it into a protected Viking settlement by surrounding it with a deep moat. After this, the warriors went on the march again, heading back down to East Anglia.

The people of East Anglia couldn't have had many horses left by this time, but it didn't matter. The Vikings weren't interested in exchanging any more horses for peace, and they didn't want Danegeld either.  Now they wanted East Anglia itself, despite the deal they'd agreed.  After killing a third king (by chopping off his head), the Vikings' great army claimed yet another victory over the shocked Anglo-Saxons.

Their dead king had been called Edmund, and his missing head was eventually found lying in woodland in Suffolk.  Edmund had been a good king, and, according to a popular legend, when his head was found it was being protected by a vicious wolf.

Vast regions of England had fallen under the Vikings' control by 878, just 13 years after the Great Heathen Army had first set sail from Scandinavia.  Having conquered East Anglia, Northumbria and most of Mercia, the Vikings now began to think about invading Wessex.

This was the richest and most powerful of the four kingdoms, and its king, Alfred the

Great, had already paid the Vikings a lot of Danegeld to leave his people alone.

This had worked at first. The Viking army had taken the Danegeld and turned back. Some of them went off to fight the people of London. Others raided parts of Scotland, and Mercia was attacked even more brutally than it had been before.

But now the Vikings were back in Wessex, and it looked as if King Alfred's only choice was to surrender to them or to order his army to fight them off. He had lost land before to the invaders, but in May 878 he fought back by launching an attack on them at the Battle of Ethandun. No one knows exactly where this important battle took place, but it may have been in what we now call Wiltshire.

King Alfred and his soldiers somehow won the battle, but the fighting was fierce and so many men on both sides were killed and injured that it wasn't a total victory. The Vikings were forced to surrender, but in return Alfred had to let them keep the land they had already conquered. This meant he was still the ruler of Wessex, but his new deal with the Vikings meant that England was suddenly split into two separate kingdoms.

The Vikings' share of it was enormous. It stretched hundreds of kilometres from London and the River Thames all the way to the River Tees, which is up near Scotland. Most of the land in the north and east was now legally Scandinavian. It was known as the Danelaw and included many towns and cities that we know today. Not just Nottingham and York but also smaller towns and villages in 15 different counties including Leicestershire, Derbyshire, Norfolk, Suffolk and Middlesex.

Everyone living in these parts of the country was now ruled by the Vikings instead of by an Anglo-Saxon king or queen. The

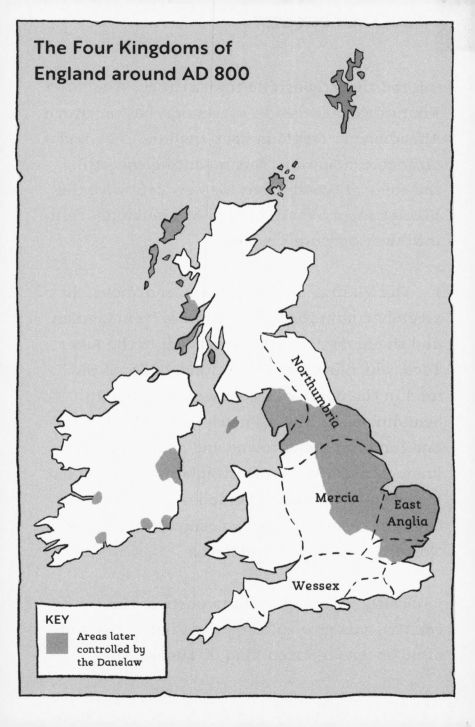

invaders also controlled Scotland's Orkney and Shetland islands and would keep control of them for many hundreds of years.

# 8

# EXPLORING THE WORLD

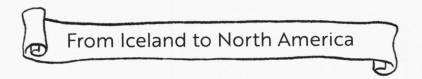

From Iceland to North America

Some Vikings continued travelling huge distances across the sea even after they had successfully conquered so much of Britain.

Their amazing longships made this possible but so did climate change. Scientists now know that the weather was warmer than normal in the ninth and tenth centuries. This reduced the number of dangerous icebergs drifting around in the Atlantic Ocean and made long voyages a bit easier.

These Vikings may have just been searching for more land that they could farm. They had managed to reach the remote Faroe Islands in the North Atlantic Ocean by the middle of the ninth century. About 20 years later, several more ships travelled even further west, to Iceland. This was more than 1,500 kilometres from the Vikings' homes in Scandinavia, which is about the same as the distance from England to Spain. Around 12,000 men, women and children eventually crossed the sea to settle in Iceland despite the difficulty and dangers of such a long journey.

Iceland was much bigger than Wessex, but nobody lived there before the Vikings. We don't know how the first Viking settlers even knew it existed, as they didn't have maps. There was no one to steal from when they arrived, so loading the first ships must have been very complicated, as they had to take everything with them that they needed to start a new life.

This meant farm animals as well as people. They also needed all the tools important for building and digging, and seeds that could be planted to grow food. Some of the longships also carried many "accidental" passengers such as mice, fleas and dung beetles.

Archaeologists have found the remains of many of these tiny creatures trapped in the Icelandic soil. This has meant scientists studying them have been able to learn a lot about the climate at this time and the first settlers' lives in their new home. For example, fleas and beetles live on animals and their dung, so their remains make it possible to work out what sort of animals the Vikings had on their farms.

Iceland was colder than Scandinavia, so farming was even harder. Some things grew fairly well, giving the settlers food to eat, but others did not. The barley crop failed to grow several times, which meant there was no beer to drink. Also, many places in the Vikings' new home weren't suitable for farming at all because Iceland has more than 30 active volcanoes.

Perhaps because of this, some of the Vikings decided to travel even further west than Iceland.  They reached Greenland, another 300 kilometres away, which was probably only discovered by accident when some Viking sailors were blown off course in a storm.

The name makes it sound like a much nicer place than Iceland, but it is actually a lot colder.  In fact, Greenland is so cold and so far from the rest of Europe that, despite being one of the largest countries in the whole world, it still has one of the smallest populations.  Even now, Greenland has only one person for every 38 square kilometres of land.  This compares to nearly 11,000 people living in 38 square kilometres of the UK.

The dangers of sailing as far as Greenland were enormous, and growing enough food in such a cold place turned out to be very difficult indeed.  Despite this, several of the Vikings

who made the journey from Iceland decided
to stay there.  One of them was called Erik
the Red, and he is believed to have gone to
Greenland after being ordered to leave Iceland
by the other Vikings.  This may have happened
after he had a violent argument with another
farmer.

Erik built a new farm in one of the most
beautiful parts of his new country as well as
a small church nearby.  This was for his wife,
who was a Christian.  The church no longer
exists, but its remains have been found by
archaeologists.

Erik eventually became the chief of all the Greenland Vikings, and he grew very rich. However, he and his family still wanted to explore more of the world, and around the year 1,000, his son Leif Eriksson set off in a longship of his own.

Leif had heard a story from another sailor who had been blown off course in a gale. This sailor said he thought he had seen yet another new land in the distance that was even further west than Greenland. Leif was fascinated by his tale, and he was determined to see if he could find it.

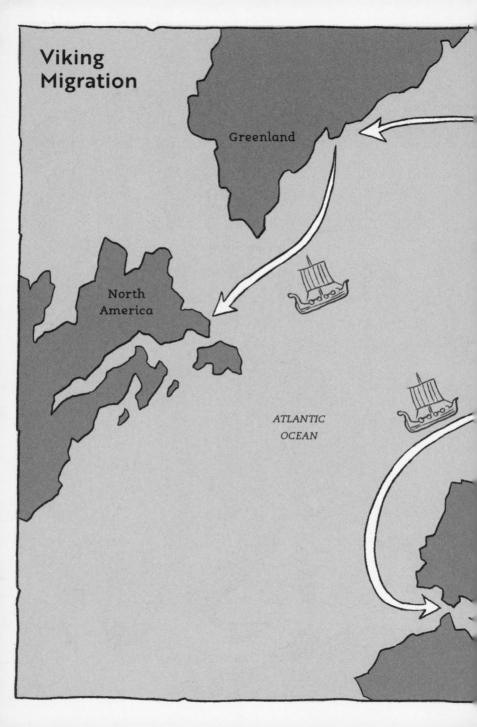

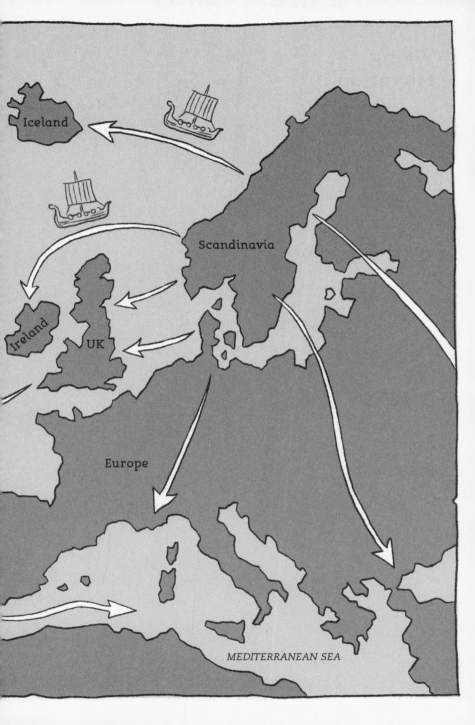

When Leif's ship finally landed there, he became the first European ever to set foot on the North American continent. The Vikings called it Vinland, meaning "wineland", possibly because grapes grew wild there. But today this is a part of Canada called Newfoundland.

Leif's discovery has led many people to think that the Vikings discovered North America, but this isn't true. Leif was brave, and his journey was certainly amazing – especially as where he landed was more than 6,000 kilometres from Scandinavia. But there were already people living there long before his ship arrived. These included Inuit hunters whose families have lived in this part of the frozen Arctic for many thousands of years.

It's impossible to know if the Inuit hunters welcomed the visitors to their land, or how friendly the Vikings were towards them. The Vikings told stories about the Inuit, saying they were all weak and scared of the Vikings.

But many Norse items have been discovered at old Inuit settlements, so it seems more likely that the two groups traded with each other before the Vikings were forced to leave.

They left because the climate changed again, and Viking farming and hunting methods simply didn't work when the weather got really, really cold. They eventually had to leave Greenland as well. This wasn't just because of the cold weather but because they had made the mistake of chopping all the trees down for wood without planting any new ones. This is something the Inuit people knew not to do.

# 9

## MAKING PEACE

Learning to Live with the Britons

By the end of the tenth century, things had also changed a lot in Britain. England's Alfred the Great had managed to stop the Vikings taking over completely, but tens of thousands of them had now arrived from Scandinavia to settle in the Danelaw as well as in Scotland, Ireland and (in much smaller numbers) in parts of south Wales. It was only after King Alfred died that some of the later kings began taking land back from the Vikings.

King Alfred's grandson Athelstan managed to recapture a lot of land in the north of

England.  Anglo-Saxon troops managed to kill the king of Jorvik, who was a Viking with the terrifying name of Erik Bloodaxe.  After this, all the Vikings living in the region had to agree to be ruled by an Anglo-Saxon king for the first time.

Many of the Viking settlers must have grown tired of fighting and were perhaps quite happy to do this.  A lot of Vikings probably wanted to live peacefully in their new country. They went back to fishing and farming and trading, and the two societies slowly began to join together.  Vikings began to give up their pagan gods to become Christians, and there were many marriages between the two different communities.  When this happened, it was impossible to say whether their children were Vikings or Anglo-Saxons.  Today we just call them English.

The same thing happened in the other places where Vikings had settled, although this

didn't stop fighting breaking out from time to time. In Ireland in 1014, the Irish managed to win the Battle of Clontarf, but when some attempts were made to invade England yet again, they were more successful.

King Sweyn of Denmark was the first to have a go. He was nicknamed "Forkbeard", and in 1013 he forced the Anglo-Saxon king to flee to France so he could rule instead. However, Sweyn mysteriously died a few weeks later, and his own son, Cnut, then became king of England.

Between 1013 and 1042 England had no fewer than four Viking kings, but when Norway's King Harald Hardrada tried to become the fifth, his attempt ended in failure.

## ENGLAND'S FOUR VIKING KINGS

**Sweyn Forkbeard**
**1013**

**Cnut the Great**
**1016–1035**

He sailed across to north-east England in 1066, but his army was soon defeated at the Battle of Stamford Bridge in Yorkshire, and King Harald Hardrada was killed. For a few weeks it seemed as if England was safe, but then yet another invading army landed on the coast of Kent.

This time the army had come from France, and it was under the command of a soldier called William of Normandy. The English army was exhausted by the Battle of Stamford Bridge

Harald Harefoot
1035–1040

Harthacnut
1040–1042

and its long march down from Yorkshire totalling 450 kilometres.

The English were soon defeated in what became known as the Battle of Hastings. William of Normandy then marched to London. On Christmas Day 1066, he was crowned King of England at Westminster Abbey. William's great-great-great-grandfather had actually been a Viking, but this marked the end of what historians call the Viking Age. A new era had begun.

# 10

# THE VIKINGS' LEGACY

Are You a Viking?

The Viking Age had lasted for less than
300 years, but most of the Vikings didn't leave
Britain when it was over.  Many Scottish
islands continued to be ruled from Norway
for several centuries (they were only returned
after the Scots' king married a Scandinavian
princess in 1469) and the Vikings' influence
can still be seen throughout Britain today.

The British still call the days of the
week after the Vikings' pagan gods Odin
(Wednesday), Thor (Thursday) and Frigg
(Friday).  There are also lots of other English

words which have Viking origins, including steak, egg, bread, fog, hug, sky and muck.

Hundreds of places in Britain have Viking names too. These include Scottish islands like Soay, Flodday and Stromay, and most towns and villages that have names ending in thorpe, toft, by, dale, keld or ness. Scarborough is another Viking name – the Yorkshire town was once ruled by a Viking called Skarth. In Scotland the name Scalpay is derived from the Viking word for an island shaped like a boat.

Lots of towns and villages also have schools and churches named after St Olaf, the patron saint of Norway. There is even a church with this name close to the Tower of London which somehow survived the Great Fire that destroyed nearly 90 other churches in 1666.

In 1852, a richly carved Viking gravestone was discovered in the churchyard of St Paul's Cathedral, and many well-preserved Viking

spears and battle-axes have been found buried
in the muddy banks of the River Thames. We
can't be sure, but these might have been the
weapons carried by the warriors of St Olaf's

army when they attacked the capital nearly a thousand years ago and pulled down London Bridge. Swords and other weapons have also been found in Scottish and Irish graves.

Perhaps the most extraordinary things left behind by the Vikings are their descendants. More than a million people living in England today have a Viking somewhere in their family tree. If you're English, you could be one of them (just like William of Normandy was), and if you live in Scotland or Ireland, the chance of your family having a Viking ancestor is even higher.